First published 2014 by Parragon Books, Ltd.
Copyright © 2018 Cottage Door Press, LLC
5005 Newport Drive, Rolling Meadows, Illinois 60008
All Rights Reserved

10 9 8 7 6 5 4 3 2 1

ISBN 978-1-68052-548-9

Written by
Steve Smallman

Illustrated by
Jaime Temairik

Parragon Books is an imprint of Cottage Door Press, LLC.
Parragon Books® and the Parragon® logo are
registered trademarks of Cottage Door Press, LLC.

TROLL

two... three... four...

PaRragon.

Trolls like to laze around
twiddling their toes,
Picking their noses, and
having a doze.

They love to creep up
behind goats and go,

"**BOO!**"

Except for one sad, lonely
troll: Boogaloo.

The other trolls tried but could not understand
Why Boogaloo felt so alone in Troll Land.
"All I want is a friend," he thought with a sigh,
And just then, a shiny red **THING** floated by!

He ran after the thing and was
running so fast,
He went straight by the sign that

NO
TROLL
SHOULD
GO PAST!

A second troll followed
behind Boogaloo,
Thinking, "Where is he going?
I want
to go,
too!"

They walked through the **KEEP-OUT** clouds straight to a place
Where a HUMAN BEING stood with a very shocked face.

The human being screamed, **"I SEE TROLLS!"** very loud,
And fled as a third troll came out of the cloud.

Another troll—number four—followed them, too, Marching in line right behind Boogaloo.

And before you could say

"boogie-boo!"

there were crowds
Of curious trolls popping out
through the clouds.

Trolls foul and furry were marching along,
Singing their favorite

troll
marching
song ...

"**Troll,** two, three, four ...

We're the trolls who **grunt** and **snore.**

Troll, two, three, four ... We don't know, there might be **more,**

But we can only count to fouuuuuurrrr!"

The humans were frightened—
the trolls looked so scary,
So scruffy and smelly, so **horrid** and **hairy!**

As the trolls passed a park, Boogaloo snuck away.
He opened the gate and he ran in to play!

In a house just nearby, a boy stood on a chair.
He whispered, **"Hey, look,** there's a troll over there!

He looks a bit lonely, I'll just go and see
If maybe he'd play with **somebody like me.**"

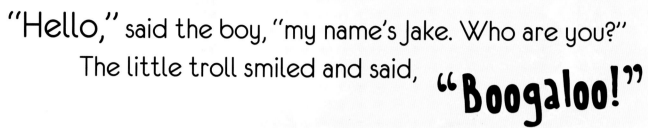

"Hello," said the boy, "my name's Jake. Who are you?"
The little troll smiled and said, **"Boogaloo!"**

"Come play on this **whizz-thing!"** Boogaloo cried.
"All right," answered Jake.
"But we call it a slide!"

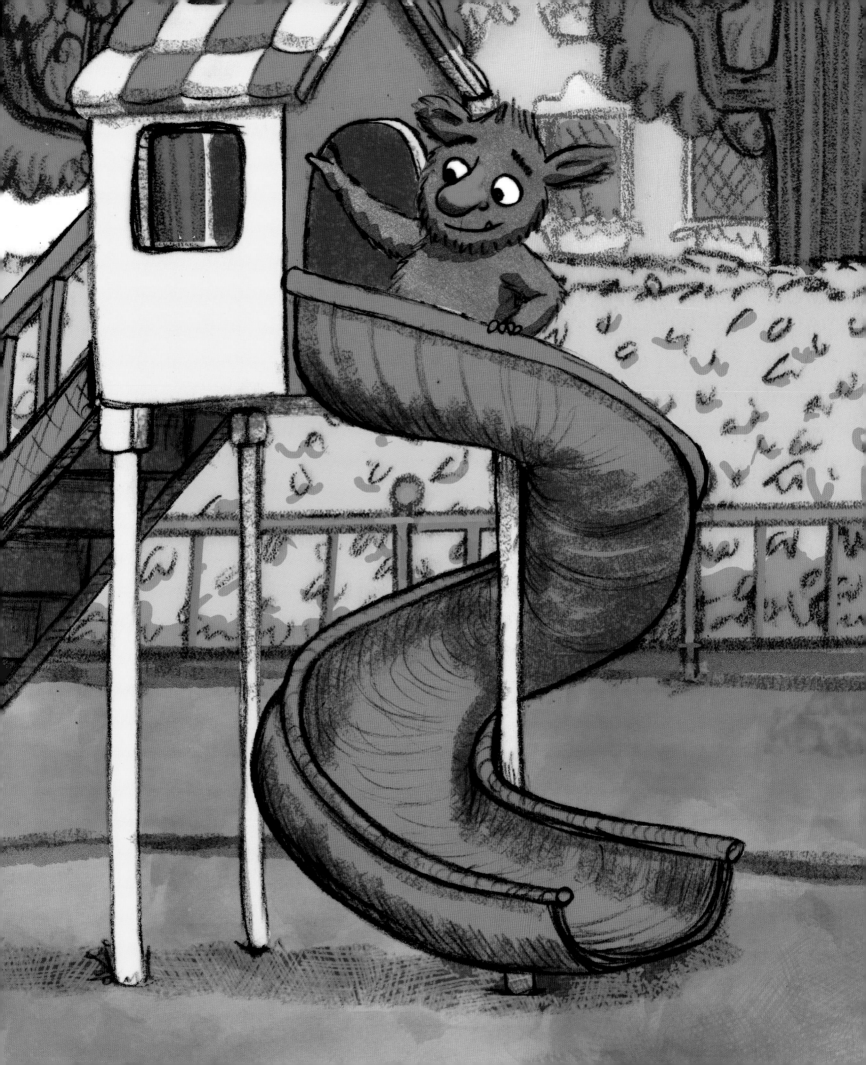

"Will you be my **very best friend**, Boogaloo?"
"Yes, please!" the troll answered.
"Will you be mine, too?"

And Humans and Trolls all crept closer to see
What **very best friends**
Trolls and Humans could be.

There is nothing between Trolls and Humans today:
The signs all came down, the clouds drifted away.
Together they play with balloons and toy boats
And no one is frightened ...

... not even
the goats!

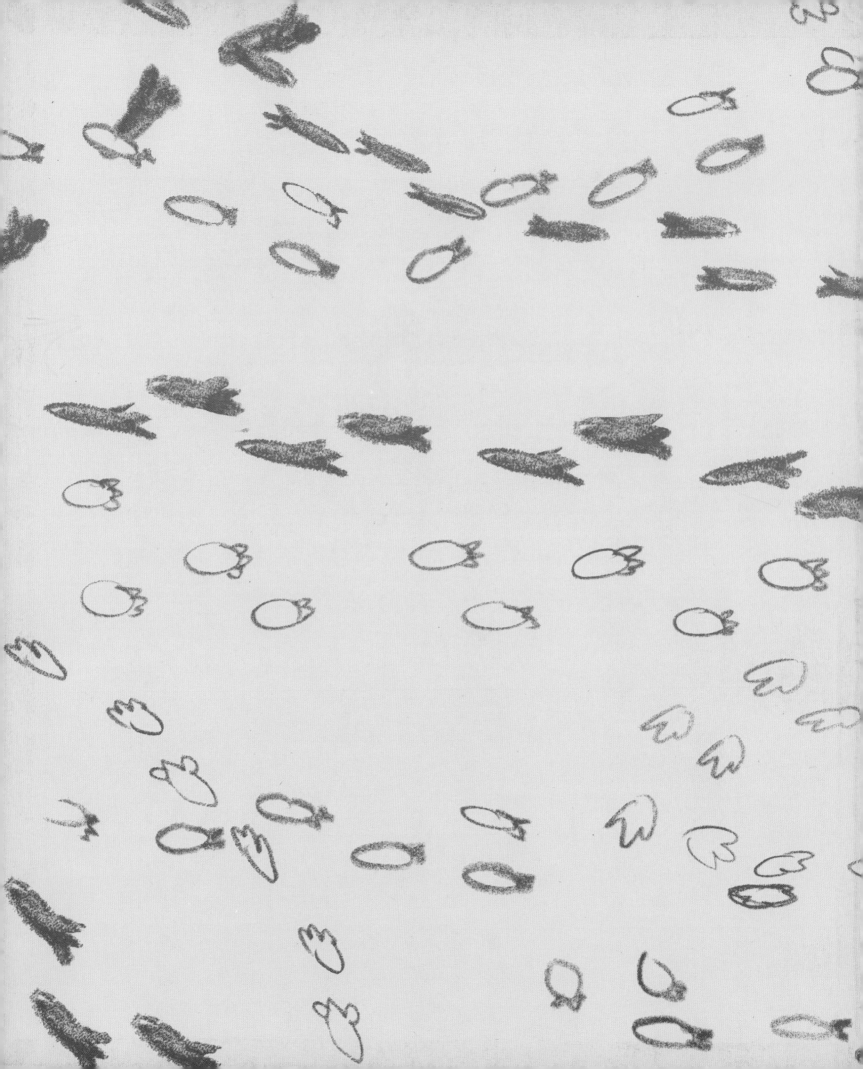